Tales of Friendship

Book 3
in the
FOX HOLLOW SERIES

Bonnie J. Gibson

Flint Hills Publishing

Original art by the author

GIBSON MADE, LLC

www.bonniejgibson.com

Cover Design by Amy Albright

STONY POINT
Graphics

Flint Hills Publishing
Topeka, Kansas

www.flinthillspublishing.com

Printed in the U.S.A.

ISBN: 978-1-953583-01-7

IN MEMORY OF

my amazing and inspiring little brother, Howard.

Down in Fox Hollow, Momma Fox's cubs, Brush and Meadow, were super excited about spring, the time of year when all the forest flowers, trees, and some of their animal friends awaken from a long winter sleep.

Momma Fox awoke early and sat down with a cup of tea. Momma Bird stopped by to talk all about her three eggs that hatched last week. While all their darlings were fast asleep, there were plenty of stories to share.

Nearby, Momma Skunk waved to the other mommas. She was already out picking flowers after enjoying the beautiful sunrise.

Soon Momma Fox could hear her cubs wrestling with the jelly jar. She excused herself so all the ladies could get on with their busy day.

After breakfast, the cubs needed to wash up for a wonderful surprise. Momma and Papa Bear had sent word that their cubs were finally awake.

Brush and Meadow loved to play with friends, especially their bear cub buddies, Rain, Brook, and River, who had been sleeping for many weeks.

Brush recalled how Rain told the funniest jokes and River was Fox Hollow's football star. Meadow could not wait to tell Brook all about her winter adventures.

As soon as the cubs went outside, they saw Gully the Turtle, with a new purple kite. Then along came Spruce Bunny and Acorn Bunny with the racoon twins Ray and Shine.

But where are the bear cubs? Brush wondered. *When will they arrive?*

"Look, Brush," squeaked Meadow, "I see them, one—two—and there is number three!"

"Yippeeeee!" hollered Brush as he turned and ran back inside to grab his football. He was so excited that he almost tripped on his own tail.

There was much hugging and a lot of high fives. It had been such a long time since they had all been together.

Brush headed straight for River, football by his side. "Come on," squealed Brush. "I've got football on my mind."

Momma Fox pulled the cubs aside. "Remember, my darlings, it is important that you find something everyone can participate in together. There's to be no child left behind."

Momma's words left Brush a little grumpy. Brush wanted to play fast and hard. But some of his friends could get hurt or slow him down, putting a damper on his fun. He did remember though, that when Meadow came over to play, she had a real knack for throwing acorns into a bowl.

Brush looked over at Gully. His chin hung down on his chest and he looked so very sad. "What's the matter, Gully?" Brush asked. Gully began to cry. Brush put his arm on Gully's shoulder, and suddenly, he had a fantastic idea!

"Hey, Gully, you're the best whistler in all of Fox Hollow."

"Yeah, so. . ." sniffled Gully.

"Well, would you like to be the referee, you know, the main animal in charge?"

Gully raised his chin up high and said, "Oh boy, would I ever!"

Momma Skunk sat her frail little darling down on a stump nearby.

Her darling's name was Little Blue because she had a patch of blue fur just above one eye. Blue was born with extra-soft muscles and found it hard to breathe sometimes. She liked to watch everyone else play. But Momma had said that everyone must participate to make sure no child was left behind.

Now Brush had a conundrum. He wasn't sure how Blue could possibly participate in a football game. Brush asked all his friends for help coming up with ideas.

Gully had a fantastic idea. He grabbed a little branch and Shine tied strips of ribbon on one side. Meadow handed the colorful branch to Blue who responded with a huge grin.

Everyone played and giggled until they were exhausted. They had so much fun they didn't even care what the score was. Every time they saw Little Blue wave her branch so high, cheering for both sides, all their hearts were filled with joy.

That night around the campfire, Brush and Meadow could not stop smiling. Brush told Momma he was very sorry for his grumpy, stubborn mind. He hadn't wanted anyone to mess up his fun game. But in the end, everything worked out fine.

Momma said, "It's time for bed, my darlings. Let's snuggle up and dream about all our friends and new adventures we'll have tomorrow."

Before he fell asleep, Brush told Momma and Meadow that his heart was full of pride. Not just because he found a way to include everyone, but for the thankful look he saw in the face of Little Blue's momma. And for Gully's head held high. And for the way everyone helped to give Blue a role from the sideline.

Thinking about all these moments brought a happy tear to Brush's eye.

"Momma?" asked Brush half asleep. "Can I ask God to help me overcome my selfish mind?

Today was just the best day ever. I always want to remember—no child left behind."

"Oh yes," said Momma, "that's a wonderful prayer for all of us."

Momma kissed Brush and Meadow on their foreheads. She told them how proud she was to be their momma. Then she hugged them really tight.

"Good night, my darlings."

"Good night, Momma."

The End.

Inspiration

This story was inspired by my amazing little brother, Dr. Howard Ray Holbrooks, and my beautiful daughter, Taylor.

Howard was a bright, spirited, boldly-athletic child. He grew into a phenomenal football player, winning accolades for both his high school and college football, academic, and military accomplishments. Howard was a rock of faith and courage in the wake of Taylor's birth with Down Syndrome and a critical congenital heart defect.

Howard went on to earn many more admirers as a husband, doctor, friend, and father. Howard left to shine his light in Heaven at the age of 44, following a valiant battle with ALS (Amyotrophic lateral sclerosis, aka Lou Gehrig's disease).

Howard finished his career as Chief of Anesthesiology at Lake Granbury Medical Center and co-owner of River Valley Anesthesia and Pain Management in Granbury, Texas. He was a proud Major in the U.S. Army and one of the biggest fans of the K.U. Jayhawks and K.C. Chiefs Kingdom. His incredible positive attitude always shined brighter than his muscular decline. I often see the tenacity in his determined face and mischievous smile when I close my eyes. He will forever be loved and never forgotten.

-Bonnie J. Gibson

Author's brother Howard with his wife Sarah and their three children: Hannah (10), Ella (2), and Jake (11) in 2010.

About the Author

The *Fox Hollow Series* is inspired by my beautiful family who has learned so much from my daughter Taylor who was born with Down Syndrome and a critical, congenital heart defect. After surviving Taylor's early childhood challenges, my family and I are navigating the very unique world of Taylor's adulthood. In this new chapter, I have become joyously aware of the healing power of creativity.

Momma, Bonnie J. Gibson

Taylor Gibson, the author's daughter

Daughter-in-law Jessalynn,
Granddaugher Emmersyn Rae, & son Brenton

The author with her husband, Jeff, & their daughter Taylor

For more about the author and her work:

www.bonniejgibson.com
Instagram@lifeacanvas
Facebook: Bonnie J. Gibson Author (@BonnieJGibson)

Don't miss books 1 & 2 in the Fox Hollow Series:
Tales of Two Cubs and *Tales at the Lake.*
Available on Amazon.com & wherever books are sold.

Made in the USA
Columbia, SC
28 August 2022

66110434R00024